www.mascotbooks.com

For more information, please contact:
Mascot Books
560 Herndon Parkway #120
Herndon, VA 20170
info@mascotbooks.com

CPSIA Code: PRT0913A
ISBN-10: 1620862921
ISBN-13: 9781620862926

Printed in the United States

THAT'S NOT OUR MASCOT?
Aubie is Our Mascot

by **Jason Wells and Jeff Wells**
illustrated by Patrick Carlson

Who's that tailgating on the Quad?

Who's that playing in the Auburn University Marching Band?

That's not our mascot...
it's Mike, the LSU Tiger.

Who's that batting
at Plainsman Park?

That's not our mascot...
it's Hairy Dawg,
the Georgia Bulldog.

Who's that leading Tiger Walk?

That's not our mascot...
it's Scratch, the Kentucky Wildcat.

Who's that rolling Toomer's Corner?

That's not our mascot...
it's Truman, the Missouri Tiger.

Who's that working out at the Rec Center?

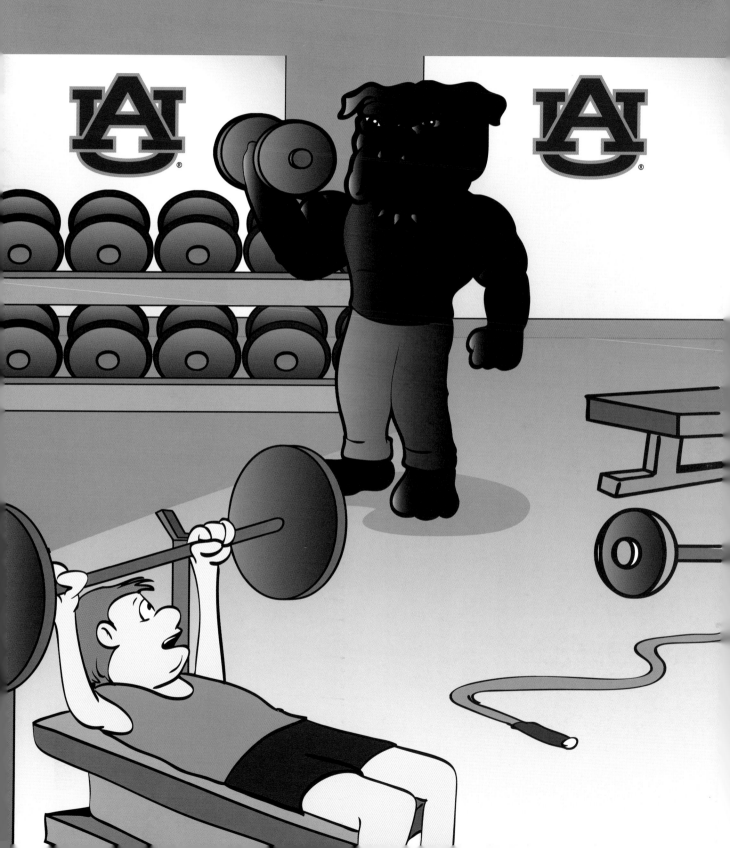

That's not our mascot...
it's Bully, the Mississippi State Bulldog.

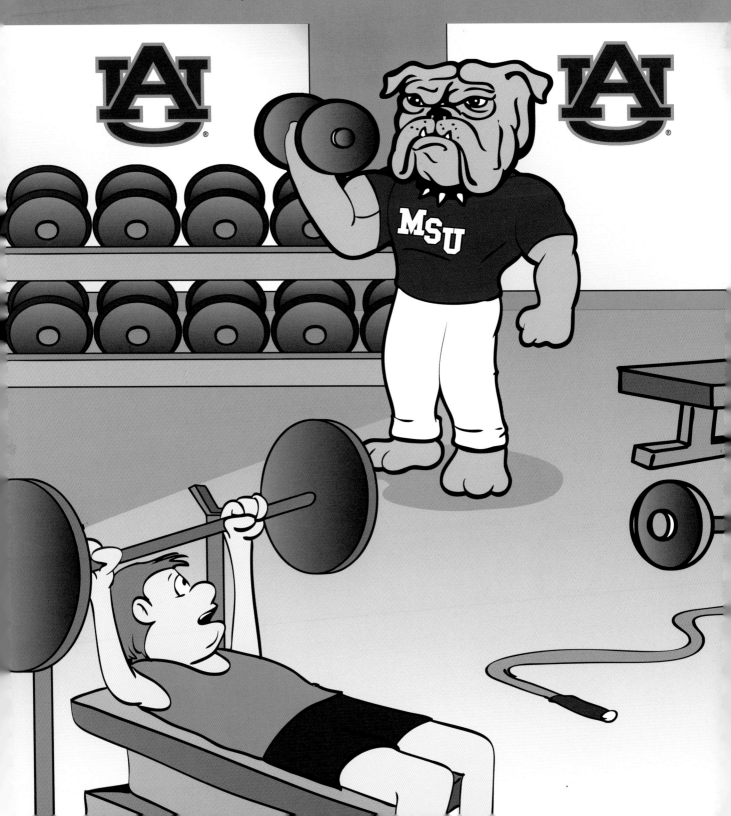

Who's that watching the eagle fly?

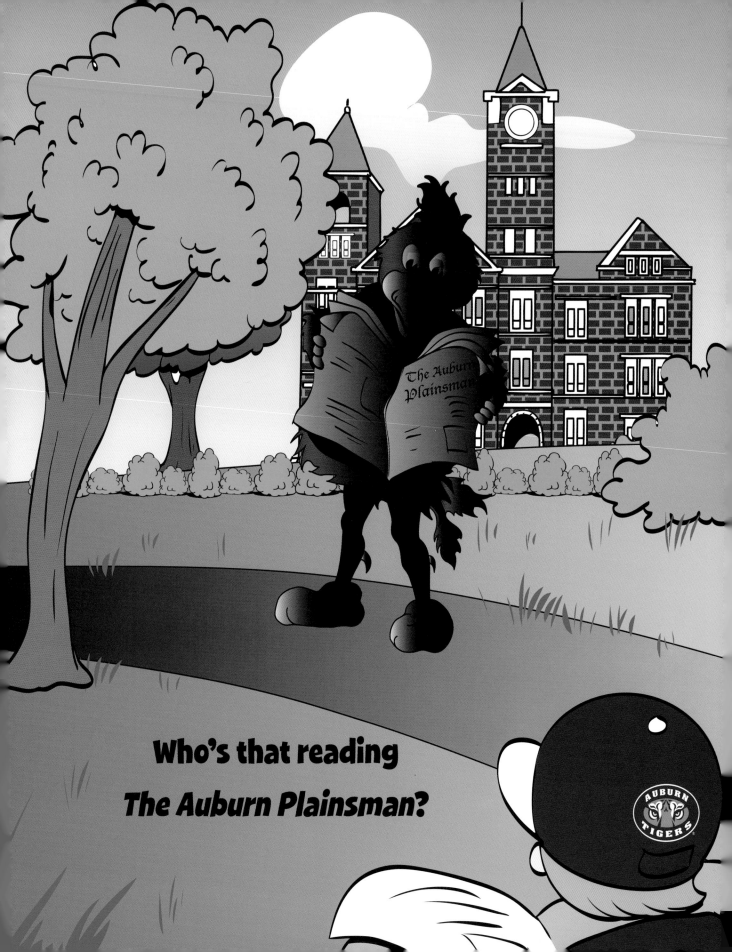

Who's that studying
at the RBD Library?

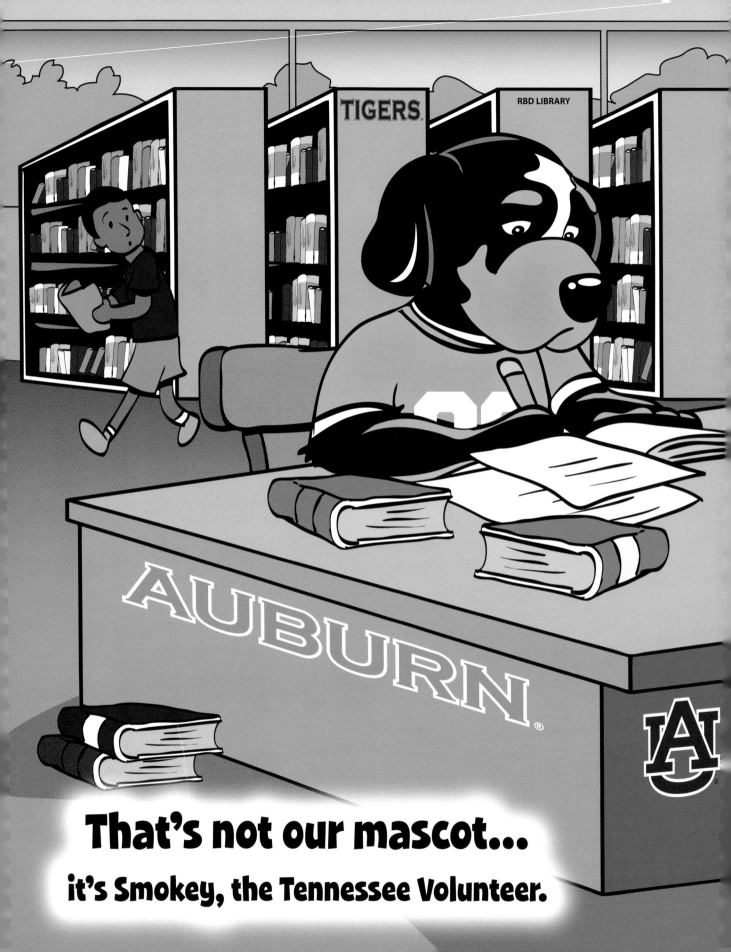

Who's that looking up
at Samford Hall?

That's not our mascot...
it's Reveille from Texas A&M.

Who's that strolling by Langdon Hall?

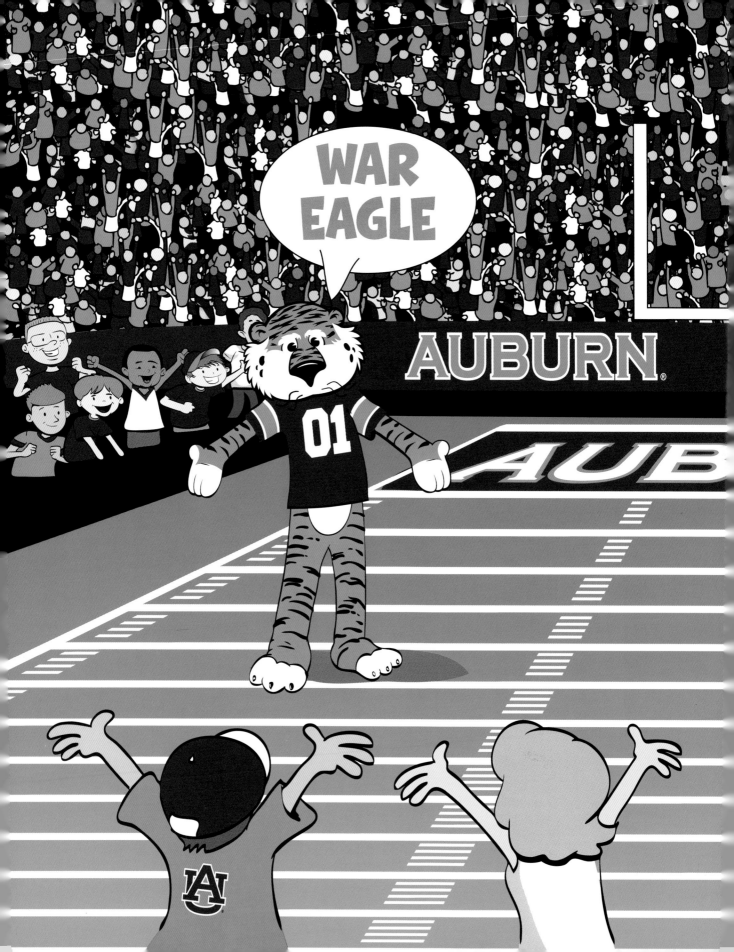